FLYNTLOCK BONES

The SCEPTRE of the PHARAOHS

For my wife, Elaine, with love
DK

For Kit
ME

First published in Great Britain in 2020 by Scallywag Press Ltd,
10 Sutherland Row, London SW1V 4JT
Text copyright © 2020 by Derek Keilty
Illustration © 2020 by Mark Elvins
The rights of Derek Keilty and Mark Elvins to be identified
as the author and illustrator of this work have been asserted by them
in accordance with the Copyright, Designs and Patents Act, 1988
All rights reserved
Edited by Deborah Chancellor
Printed and bound in Great Britain by Clays Ltd, Elcograf S.p.A.
Printed on FSC paper
001
British Library Cataloguing in Publication Data available
ISBN 978-1-912650-40-8

FLYNTLOCK BONES

The SCEPTRE of The PHARAOHS

By Derek Keilty

Illustrated by Mark Elvins

Scallywag Press Ltd
LONDON

The Seven Seas

Dire Straits

Mystic Sea

Bohemia

Cutlass Sea

Shark Sea

Calcutlass Island

Sharktooth Island

GALLERY of CHARACTERS

The Black Hound

Flynn

Red

Cap'n Watkins

Briggs

Drudger

Hudson

Scratch

The Twins

Fishbreath

The Scurvy Serpent

Cap'n Morihearty

Dog bite

Gypshun Museum

Dr Khan

Miss Wrinkly

Miss Chatti

CHAPTER ONE
THE BLACK HOUND

Creak! Squawk!! Creak!!!

My heart flutters as I stride up the gangplank of the tall sailing ship that lurches and creaks in the harbour. There's a loud crack of thunder and I slip, almost plunging head first into the murky sea that is swirling round the ship's hull. I hope the sailor in the crow's nest hasn't got a spyglass

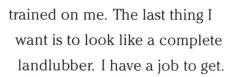

trained on me. The last thing I want is to look like a complete landlubber. I have a job to get.

Going back to the orphanage is not an option anymore. Mrs Wiggins the Matron practically chucked me out on my ear this morning, saying I'm too old now for mollycoddling. She says it's high time I was out working for a living, making my own way in the world. Mollycoddling! The cheek of her, when it was me that did all the shopping, washing and cleaning, for which, I might add, she never gave me a penny.

At the top of the gangway, a gruff voice calls out.

'Ahoy there! What scuttling sea rat gets aboard the Black Hound without my knowing?'

I freeze as a big, burly man looms over me, silhouetted in the sunlight. Squinting up at him, I can't help but notice he has not one, but two eye patches, covering both his eyes. He is wearing a black hat and has the bushiest beard I have ever seen. My heart hammers even harder and I swallow an anchor-sized throat lump. I have only ever read stories about pirates and seen maybe a picture or two in books, so I'm no expert... But the man standing in front of me is the spitting image of a pirate – and I have a sudden cold fear that the boat I've boarded might be a real pirate ship!

'I'm...I'm here about the job, sir,' I stutter, struggling to keep my voice steady. I am struck by the thought he might knock me flying, right then and there, putting an end to my hopeless

job hunt before it even began. What would Mrs Wiggins think then?

'Job. What job?'

'The one advertised in Mrs Bunn's bakery.' I fish out the card I'd taken this morning when buying bread for the orphanage. There had been a whole pile of them. It reads:

Cabin Boy wanted
for the Black Hound.
Apply at Baskervile Harbour.

'I don't see any card. What are you talking about, lad?'

'Yer eye patches,' I point out to him with a nervous chuckle.

He flips up one of the patches. A pale blue

eye blinks down at me.

'Ah, there y'are. I were havin' a bit of shut eye before we set sail.' He takes the card and stuffs it in his pocket.

'Y'are a bit on the scrawny side for a cabin boy. It's hard work, y'know.' He peers at me and grins hopefully. 'Don't suppose ya brought anything from the bakery? Mrs Bunn makes the best hot pies I ever tasted!'

I notice a tall man striding across the deck. It is the ship's captain, it must be. He is wearing a three-cornered hat, a long coat, ruffled shirt, pants, boots, and a cutlass on his belt. And he has a nose like a beak.

'What's all the fuss about, Briggs?'

'There be a lad 'ere, Cap'n, looking for a job.'

'Well don't just stand there, bring him aboard.' He straightens his hat and beckons to us. 'I'll see him in my quarters right now. Must say I was beginning to wonder if anyone was going to show up. You did remember to leave all those cards around the shops in town, didn't you Briggs?'

'Er… aye, Cap'n.'

My heart leaps. And though I am worried that it is a job aboard a pirate ship, I balance it with the fact that a job is a job. And surely it couldn't be any worse than skivvying for Mrs Wiggins.

I follow the patch-wearing Briggs across the deck to the open door of a cabin, where the Captain waves for me to enter.

'Come in. Come in!'

Inside, the cabin is large and gloomy, almost the size of the dormitories at the orphanage. The first thing I notice is a bookcase by the window, crammed with all kinds of volumes. There's a desk too, cluttered with candles, maps, a pipe, and a magnifying glass. And in the corner, a grinning skeleton, holding a violin, and a single brown slipper containing a pouch of tobacco.

'Captain Long John Watkins o' the Black

Hound, and you might be?' says the Captain,
extending a hand.

'Flyntlock Bones, sir, o' the good town of
Baskervile. Though most folks call me Flynn.
Pleased to meet you.'

He pulls out a stool for me, then strides
round to recline on a wooden rocking chair. A
scrawny black cat with a matted coat and one
eye leaps up on the table to lie by the Captain's
hand. It stares at me, almost like it knows what

I am thinking – like it knows all about me.

'What's your cat's name, Captain Watkins?' I ask.

He gives her a rub between the ears with a grimy finger.

'Scratch. She's the hardest worker on this ship. Keeps the mice and rats away from all the sacks o' grub down in the hold.'

'What happened to her eye?'

'You'll have to ask her that one yourself.' He grins. 'One of the crew picked her up a few years ago on an island in the Dire Straits. She was in pretty bad shape. We took her in, fed her and she's been with us ever since.'

'I always wanted a cat, but I was never allowed one.'

The Captain fiddles with his pipe, reaching over to take the tobacco pouch from his slipper.

'About the job, young Flynn. Y'ever been to sea before?'

'Not till today, Sir.'

'It's tough work y'know, tougher if you have to learn everything from scratch, too.' He glances at the cat. 'Not this Scratch, of course.'

'Wouldn't expect anything less, sir but I picks things up real quick, so I does, so you've nothing to worry about there.'

'Your parents OK with you going to sea?'

'I'm an orphan, sir. My folks died in the great fire of Baskervile when I was a baby. They say it's a miracle I survived.'

'Sorry to hear that, lad. Then you live at the orphanage?'

'Not anymore. Mrs Wiggins the Matron all but kicked me out only this morning, sir. That's why I needs a job.'

11

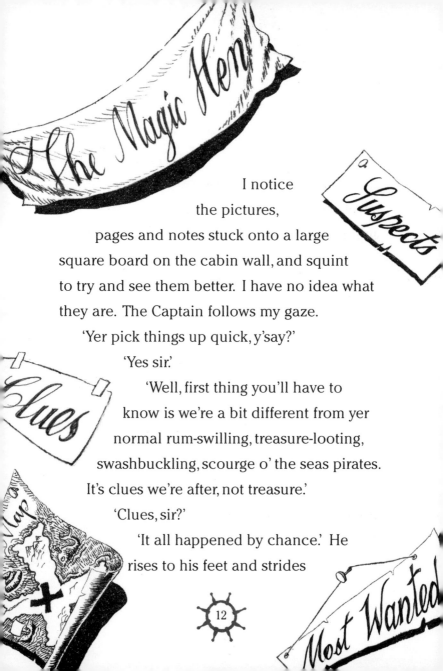

I notice
the pictures,
pages and notes stuck onto a large
square board on the cabin wall, and squint
to try and see them better. I have no idea what
they are. The Captain follows my gaze.

'Yer pick things up quick, y'say?'

'Yes sir.'

'Well, first thing you'll have to
know is we're a bit different from yer
normal rum-swilling, treasure-looting,
swashbuckling, scourge o' the seas pirates.
It's clues we're after, not treasure.'

'Clues, sir?'

'It all happened by chance.' He
rises to his feet and strides

over to the board. 'A few years back we hit a bit of a lean patch. Treasure were getting harder and harder to find. Then one day we came upon a rich countess in a tavern in Bohemia, with a tale of woe about her stolen jewels. Proper sobbing her heart out she was. Telling the whole tavern how priceless they were, and that pirates were most likely to blame. Obviously, she had no idea she was in the company of a whole band of 'em, on account of us being with her in the same establishment.'

He chuckles and puts a match to his pipe, puffing and blowing at it until I am pretty sure it has gone out. Unperturbed, he places it gently back on the desk.

'Said she'd tried everything, including the local constabulary, who were next to useless. Anyways, an idea popped into my head and I asked if there would be a reward for the safe return of her jewels, to which the countess replied there would. And, yo ho ho, our first ever investigation. We set sail, procuring the stolen booty from old Scarletbeard, resident pirate of Sharktooth Island – sneaked them away in the dead of night, when he was out celebrating his ill-gotten gains. So we brought the jewels back to their rightful owner – though I confess I did think about putting them in our own pitilessly empty booty chest. 'Course my honesty paid off with a handsome reward. The countess told her friends about me and it weren't long before we set sail on our second case. The rest, as they say, is history. So you see, this job en't just for a cabin boy, young Flynn. It's for a cabin boy aboard a ship full o' the cleverest pirate investigators ya ever set eyes upon.'

He pauses. 'You OK, lad? Ya gone paler than a full moon.'

While the Captain had been speaking, I'd come over a bit dizzy. I had hoped that concentrating on the story would have made me feel better, but it hadn't.

'It's not that sir, just feel a bit queasy, that's all.'

'Ah sea sick then. Been a landlubber too long, and this choppy weather won't help very much.'

'Reckon it's just nerves, on account of me needing this job so very much.'

He pours a glass of water and hands it to me.

I wish it weren't so stormy today. I take a sip and clear my throat.

Then everything goes the darkest shade of black.

CHAPTER TWO
THE MAGIC HEN

I open my eyes to find myself slumped on the Captain's desk, head cradled on one arm. Scratch is curled up by the brass spyglass. One eye staring at me.

Why is it so quiet? Where is the Captain?

I lift my head, which pounds like a drum. How long have I been out cold? The storm seems to have calmed a lot. Scratch and me are the only occupants of the cabin. I figure I'll hardly get the job now. I don't know much about what a cabin boy does, let alone what a cabin boy on a ship full of pirate investigators does, but I had already made up my mind that it looked like a lot more fun than all the chores Mrs Wiggins had me doing at the orphanage,

till my fingers were worn to the bone. I stare at the cabin wall, the one with the board on it, and not really knowing why, I wander over to read the pages and look at the drawings.

I am curiously drawn to it all. It reminds me of the jigsaw puzzles I used to do in the orphanage, as pages of different sizes and shapes are pinned next to each other so closely. But it doesn't make a mite of sense to me.

A banner at the top reads:

The Magic Hen

Below the banner are smaller headings, like 'Suspects', 'Clues', 'Most Wanted', and 'Mission Map'. Arrows connect some of the pages, and there are notes with scribbles on them, pinned on like an afterthought.

I fetch the magnifying glass and try to read them. I wish I could understand what it all means and who the people in the pictures are. I've no idea what the scribbled notes are about, as most are in squiggly handwriting that could easily be a foreign language. Some of the crew are from far flung parts of the Seven Seas, where they speak different languages. The more I study it, the more I realise the mystery surrounds a stolen hen. But not just any old hen. A magic hen that lays a golden egg once a year. Seems most folks reckon it's all nonsense, apart from one sneak thief who thought it likely enough to break in and steal the hen one night.

'Who do you reckon stole it, Scratch?'

Scratch blinks up at me with her one good eye, stretches and meows, then falls back to sleep. I grin.

'Thanks for your help.'

Next thing, the door bursts open and I almost jump out of my skin. Captain Watkins comes steaming in, his neck-tie flapping.

'Yer be awake then, young Flynn. You OK?'

'Yes, sir. Sorry, sir. Came over a bit faint, that's all. I'm fine now.'

He pours me a fresh glass of water, then takes off his hat and sits down in the rocking chair. I walk over to sit opposite him.

'Put me in a pickle, you have, my lad.'

I take a sip of water.

'Pickle, how?'

'You understand I can't be having a seasick cabin boy about the Hound?'

'It won't happen again, Captain, I promise it won't.'

'But you won't know see, that's the thing with seasickness. It creeps up on ya like a sea monster's tentacle. And we're making ready to set sail.'

'I'm fine. It was… I don't know what came over me. I'm a good worker, you'll see if you give me a chance.'

I feel sick, only this time it isn't sea sickness. Where will I go if I can't go back to the orphanage? If Mrs Wiggins really has booted me out for good, like she threatened to, what am I going to do?

I notice that Scratch has slinked over to what looks like her favourite spot, on a chair below the board. A clever thought suddenly strikes me.

'I...I was looking at your display,' I blurt out.

His eyebrows leap up his forehead.

'Ah, you were, were you. And there's me thinking you were out for the count.'

'I believe you're trying to find a precious magic hen, and have three main suspects?'

'Led us a merry dance round the Seven Seas, that case did,' he sighs. 'Like headless chickens, if you'll pardon the pun.'

'If I was you, I'd think about having a word with the butcher's son, Jack Brown.'

22

The Captain strokes his chin, his eyes flitting between me and the information board.

'Why do you say that?' he asks.

I lift the magnifying glass from the desk and stride over to the board.

'When I was looking at his picture...' I hold the magnifying glass over the breast pocket of the young man's coat. 'Right there. See. There's a chicken feather sticking out of the pocket of his suit.'

The Captain's eyebrows leap up for a second time.

'Reckon you got a knack for solving cases, do you?'

'En't solved yet Captain, I was just thinking you might go talk to him.'

23

'And what if I told you we already have?'

'You have?'

'Caught him two days ago, trying to escape aboard a ship with the

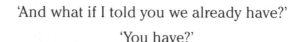

magic hen. He's now having a well-earned rest, courtesy of Baskervile prison. The case you were looking at was our last case. We just haven't had a chance to clear up the board yet.'

'I see sir. I didn't know.'

As I speak, Briggs sticks his head in at the door.

'Bosun's waiting for yer order to raise the anchor, Cap'n.'

'Tell him to hoist away, Master Briggs, and I'm on my way to the helm.'

The Captain gets to his feet and fixes me with a stare.

'You're determined, I'll give you that, and smart too. The crew of the Black Hound needs thinkers as well as doers, and I reckon yer might be a bit o' both.'

I watch as he lifts his hat, dusting it down. He strides to the door. My heart thuds, but I say nothing.

At the door he turns and gives me a wink.

'You'll have a week's trial, young Flynn, to see if you can find them sea legs o' yours.'
I gasp.

'I will sir. Promise I will.'

CHAPTER THREE
RED

A hot sun beams down on my face where I stand on the deck of the Black Hound. Around me the crew have all sprung into action, hoisting sails, climbing ropes, rolling barrels along the deck, disappearing down wooden hatches.

'All hands about ship!' Briggs yells.

Everybody knows what to do except me, and Captain Watkins left me ages ago, or at least it seems like it, to go and steer the ship. But I don't care. I couldn't be happier. I'd got myself a job. And that meant I wasn't going back to Baskervile Orphanage any time soon.

Suddenly, a voice calls out, 'Hey down there!'

I spin round but there's no one there, only the ship's main mast, towering into the sky. Then I feel something hit my head.

'Up here!'

I look up to see a red-haired girl with a grubby face, about my own age, grinning down at me from the mast.

'Hey, new boy. You bin to sea before?' she calls. I shake my head.

'En't been anywhere 'cept the town where I was born.'

'So, you never been on a ship then?'

'Not till today.'

She glances past me and I follow her gaze to where Captain Watkins stands proudly, shoulders back, at the helm. I think I see him give her a nod.

'Then you best follow me.'

'Follow you where?'

'Crow's nest. S'where your training begins.' And she's off, climbing the rope ladder like a chimpanzee. 'Maybe you'll stick around longer than our last cabin boy.'

'Why, what happened to him?'

She doesn't answer. I watch her climb higher, feeling a lump rise in my throat. Then I see the Captain, who in between barking orders at the crew, glances over in my direction. I feel scared, but I know I have to make a move, especially with the Captain watching. So I take a deep breath, and start to climb the ladder.

'What's your name?' I shout up to her.

'Red,' she calls back. 'On account o' me flamin' red hair. What's yours?'

'Flynn.'

'Ya got folks, Flynn?'

'Died in the Great Fire of Baskervile.'

'Sorry 'bout that. I'm an orphan myself. My Mum died when I was a tot and Dad died in a shipwreck. He was a fisherman.'

My arms ache and my knees feel like two jellies. I wonder how far we have climbed, though I daren't look down. The wind howls and the noise of the flapping sails is deafening.

'Ya done any work before?' Red asks.

'Scuttled up a few chimney stacks in Baskerville when I was small. And I skivvied plenty for Mrs Wiggins at the orphanage, 'fore she threw me out. She was the Matron.'

Red just keeps on climbing, higher, higher. She makes it look effortless, but I have to watch every step, in case I miss a rope or slip. At the top of the mast, we climb into the barrel-shaped crow's nest.

The view is breathtaking. On one side the Bellgravyan Sea shimmers for miles to the horizon. And on the other, the shoreline and the rooftops of Baskervile are getting smaller as we sail farther out to sea.

'It's… it's amazing!'

'I love it up here, looking at the sky. S'even better at night. You can see the stars so much clearer at sea than in the city, what with all them torches and lanterns.'

'How long have you been on this ship?'

'About a year now. Before that I was apprenticed to an old witch on an island in the Mystic Sea, where I was born. But I didn't care much for spells and potions, so I ran away.' I gasp.

'You mean, you could've been a witch?'

'Doubt it. The old crow wanted to dye my
hair jet black like hers, and I wasn't having any
of it. So I scarpered, first chance I got.'

'Don't blame you.'

'OK, first lesson: ship bits!' Red
says, slapping a hand on the
thick wooden pole with the
ship's flag at the top – a
skull and crossbones, only
with a magnifying glass
over one bony eye socket.
'There are two masts. This
here's the main mast, and
to the bow of the ship is
the foremast.'
I frown.

'Bow?'

'The front of the ship

is called the bow and the
back is called the stern.
The main deck is where we
climbed from, leading up to
the quarter deck. And the

Captain's cabin is beneath the poop deck.'
I chuckle.

'There's a poop deck?'

'Not that sort of poop.' She grins, rolling
her eyes. 'And below deck is called the hull.
I'll show you, later. You'll be down there a lot
helping ol' Fishbreath, the ship's cook. You'll
need your wits about you with him mind, as he
gets a bit grouchy.'

'I see. But the Captain seems friendly
enough.' Red nods.

'Captain Watkins is a genius. The way he
can solve a crime or a mystery or a puzzle –
never met anyone like him. Master o' disguise
he is, too.'

'Disguise?'

'Aye, you've maybe passed an old woman selling flowers in the market place, not knowing it's been the Cap'n the whole time. Maddening too though, as sometimes he'll have us all in his cabin and we'll all be staring blankly at the clues stuck on the cabin wall. Then he'll reveal the culprit and I'm like, wow, I see it now, but wish I'd thought of it sooner.'

'So you help with the investigation cases?'

'Cap'n expects the whole crew to help solve the crimes. He says that aboard the Black Hound we're all pirate investigators working together. We've had a few close calls, and a

few sea monsters too.' She frowns at me. 'You alright, Flynn? You've gone a funny colour.'

I don't tell her, but the feeling I had earlier is starting to come back.

'I'm fine.'

'It's OK, the roll of the ship is ten times worse in the crow's nest.' She smiles. 'Even Briggs gets sick up here and he's got guts of iron. Come on, we're done here anyways, and I want to show you something below deck. You'll want to see where you'll be sleeping tonight.'

As we descend, I start to feel better and breathe a deep sigh of relief.

'So apart from helping solve cases, what else will I be doing?' I ask.

'All sorts of things: swabbing the decks, trimming the sails, cleaning the quarters, washing clothes, serving meals, running errands, learning knots and splices, not to mention steering the ship.'

'Steering the ship? Y'mean like the Cap'n?'

'Not today of course, but you will one day.'

Back on deck, Red clasps me tight on the arm.

'Good job, Flynn. Now it's time to meet the crew.'

I notice that over her shoulder a band of shipmates are heading toward us. I wonder if maybe the crew have decided to come and meet us first. But instead they push past us in a hurry. I look up and notice that the Captain is no longer standing at the helm but has been replaced by a skinny pirate.

'Crew are all wanted in the Captain's cabin, sharpish, Red,' one of them grunts. 'And best

bring yer new friend, too.'

'Aye, sir.' Red salutes him then gives me a nudge. 'Let's go. Captain's called a meeting.'

'A meeting about what?' I ask, feeling like I'm asking far too many questions.

'Captain can call a meeting whenever he likes,' Red sniffs. 'Mind you, calling a meeting when we've only just set sail usually means one thing.'

'What?'

Arriving at the wooden cabin door, Red turns, her face suddenly beaming, her eyes wide with excitement.

'We got us a case to investigate.'

CHAPTER FOUR
THE BREAK-IN

The Captain's cabin is crammed full of crew members of all shapes and sizes. Some are perched on barrels, others gathered around the Captain's desk. I squeeze in to stand by the bookcase, feeling a lot of pirate eyes gawking at me. Scratch wanders over to nuzzle my leg, then curls up at my feet.

Captain Watkins sits behind the desk, straightening his three-cornered hat, waiting for everyone to settle. Finally, he hammers his pipe on the desk, clearing his throat.

'Now listen up hearties, it don't take a pirate investigator to work out that there's one extra crew member in attendance at this 'ere meeting. So I'd like to introduce you all to our new cabin boy, Flyntlock Bones, o' the town o' Baskervile.'

The crew look me up and down like I'm a sort of weird zoo animal, one that they haven't seen before.

'Course now he's already met the most handsome, and cleverest crew member.' The Captain smirks, tweaking his moustache in the mirror. 'So I think it only proper we go round the circle and you all introduce yourselves.'

'Hope he en't a picky eater. Nothin' I hates more than picky eaters!' growls a meaty-faced pirate with a drooping moustache and wild eyebrows. I notice he is missing a hand, but he doesn't have a hook like most pirates, instead he has a large silver spoon.

'Name's Fishbreath, lad,' he says. 'You'll have the pleasure of dining on me dried beef and hardtack soon enough, just make sure you keep an eye out for weevils.'

'Best eatin' them in the dark,' Red adds with a wide grin. 'That way, what you can't see won't harm ya.'

Briggs pipes up next, running a hand through his beard.

'I've squared up to this lad to welcome him aboard, so I s'pose we've already met, too. I'm the ship's quartermaster, which means I keep you scurvy lot in order. So I'll be keepin' ya busy, young Flynn.'

A barrel-shaped pirate with stubby legs and a parrot on his shoulder tips his hat to me.

'Pleased to meet ya lad. I'm Master Hudson, the ship's bosun, in charge of everything that keeps us afloat and heading the right way.'

'I'm Red, ship's rigger.' Red gives me a wink then she nudges the boy beside her in the ribs.

'The name's Snitch, and this ere's my twin brother, Dedweird.'

I wonder if that is everyone, then I notice a shadowy figure hunched in the corner of the cabin, like he is trying to keep out of the way. A boy maybe a few years older than me, with a dirty face and dark eyes.

'Scratch got your tongue?'
The Captain drums his fingers.
'Hurry up, we haven't got
all day.'

'Drudger, ship's
rigger,' he mumbles, not even
bothering to look up.

'Right, now down
to business,' says the
Captain. 'A parrot has
flown aboard with a

message all the way from
the Isle of Tut. A letter
from a client enquiring
after our services.'

Unfolding the
crumpled paper,
he reads it
aloud, his brow
furrowing.

Dear Captain Watkins.

My name is Miss Kristina Wrinkly, curator of the Gypshun Museum. My museum was broken into last night and ransacked. A band of merciless thieves smashed up display cabinets, destroyed exhibits and stole priceless, ancient artefacts, including the irreplaceable Sceptre of the Pharaohs. The place is in a dreadful mess. I don't know what to do, and I am frightened they might return. I have heard that you and your crew are the best investigators on the Seven Seas, so I did not think twice about sending a parrot in the hope that you can help me.

I listen attentively, glancing round at the rest of the crew. All have serious expressions on their faces. Hudson scratches his head. Briggs scribbles notes in a little notebook.

'So it seems we have a gang of thieves operating on what is usually a quiet part of the Seven Seas, the ancient Isle of Tut,' says the Captain, pointing to a map on the board. I notice that all the papers from the last case have now been taken down.

Fishbreath frowns.

'Wouldn't like to be in their shoes. Reckon a lot of them Gypshun treasures are cursed. I once heard a story about a pirate raiding the tomb of an ancient Gypshun king, but when he got inside, the whole thing caved in on him. Some say he's still buried in there with the mummies.'

'Probably a mummy himself by now,' says Hudson. Briggs nods.

'Could get more than they bargained for, stealin' ancient booty.'

'Can't recall a case that's started out with such an urgent plea for help,' says the Captain. 'Reckon we take this one on and get to work sharpish. Briggs, you'll plot us a course for the Isle of Tut. How long yer reckon it'll take us?'

'Fair winds should get us there by dawn, Captain.'

I feel a rush of excitement. This is it. My first case. I have heard stories that there are

pyramids the size of mountains on the Isle
of Tut, and now I'm actually going there. Mrs
Wiggins would scarcely believe it, I'm sure.

The crew file out of the cabin and the
Captain turns to me.

'Looks like yer gonna get a chance to prove
that knack for solving cases, young Flynn.
You up for it?'

'Aye, sir. I won't let you down.'

'Well said, lad. Saw you in the crow's nest
earlier, too. There's hope for them sea legs o'
yours yet.' He grins then breezes out of the door.

CHAPTER FIVE
VOYAGE TO TUT

Later, I stand on the quarter deck waiting for Red, who has gone to help secure the top sail.

I think about Miss Wrinkly's cry for help and it dawns on me that I have never really helped anyone before. Except at the orphanage, when my friend's pet mouse got caught inside one of

Mrs Wiggins armchairs. I was terrified the old battleaxe would notice the cut I made under the seat and go nuts with me for ruining her good furniture.

'No time for gaping out to sea, Bones,' a voice booms. 'There's work to be done 'fore we get to the Isle of Tut.' I spin round to see Briggs holding a bucket and mop, grinning a toothless grin.

'Cap'n likes a nice clean ship, only it don't

clean itself. Swabbing the deck is one of the main chores o' the cabin boy.'

'Aye, sir. Don't worry, sir.' I take the bucket from him. 'I'll have the place ship shape in no time, you wait an' see.'

He grunts and plods off and I plunge the mop into the bucket of water. I don't mind hard work. I know this isn't a holiday. Besides, I used to do mopping at the orphanage. And I've got to show the Captain I'm as good as my word – with only a week to do it.

I get to work swabbing the deck. It's hard work and sweaty, too. The sun is getting hotter all the time as it rises in the sky.

'Be there all day doing it that way.' I look up to see a grimy face with dark eyes. It's the surly boy from the cabin.

'Drudger. Hello.'

'Best to pour the water over the deck first, then brush it.'

'But I haven't got a brush,' I say. 'Just a mop.'

'But I haven't got a brush,' he mimics with a sneer. 'They're in the store.'

'I'm afraid I don't know where that is.'

'Don't know much. Be surprised you even know how to pour water. But don't worry, I can help.' And he kicks over the bucket, the water spilling over the deck.

'Oops, sorry.'

'Hey, you done that on purpose!'
I protest.

He grabs me by the shirt and lifts me up.

I can see right inside his mouth, and his breath smells like week-old socks.

'Look Bones, I'm doing you a favour. Now you know how to swab the deck properly, and when you're getting more water you can get a brush, too. And if yer not careful, I'll swab the deck with you.'

Next thing, Red swings down from the rigging like a trapeze artist.

'I saw that, Drudger, and I've half a mind to tell the Captain. It's the boy's first day, so leave him be.'

'I'm OK,' I say.

'Saw what?' moans Drudger. 'I was only trying to help. Oh well, I'm off then.' And he climbs the rigging and disappears out of sight.

'C'mon I'll show you where the water barrel is,' Red says.

'Drudger can be a right bully. He's sore that we en't piratin' anymore. Told me he hates all this investigatin' and doesn't know why we can't just be pirates again. Thinks the Captain's mad for changing. O'course he'd never say that to his face, or the Captain would make him walk the plank. Watkins has still got pirate in 'im yet.'

Later, we eat dinner down in the ship's hold. The kitchen is small and cramped and there is a metal box of sand

55

with coals burning in the middle. Fishbreath is busily stirring a pot of soup on the fire for the Captain, using his spoon hand. He gives me a grunt, handing over a piece of dried beef and what looks like a hard biscuit. I wonder if there are any weevils in it.

'This water tastes funny,' I tell Red. 'How long's it been in that barrel?'

Red gasps.

'Flynn. Which barrel have you been filling your cup from?'

I point. 'That one over there.'

'Perishin' parrots, that's the grog!'

'Grog. What's grog?'

'Pirate beer. You're meant to drink the water from the other barrel.'

Just then Drudger pushes past me.

'You again. Watch where yer goin', bone face!' he spits.

'Why don't you wash where yer goin',

Booger,' I slur.

'What did you call me?'

'I mean Bodger. I mean... I'm not sure what I mean.' I feel very woozy.

'I'll bash your beak nose till it's as flat as the rest of your ugly mug.'

Drudger clenches his fists, his eyes, his teeth. It's like he's clenching everything, probably even his bum cheeks.

I decide now might be a good time to run for it. But my legs don't seem to be doing what I want them to do. I stagger up the wooden stairs, hearing Drudger close behind me.

On deck, I turn round and see Drudger reach the top of the stairwell. He looms toward me, leering like a mad hyena.

I stumble backwards, expecting in my befuddled mind that I'll eventually back into the rail that skirts the edge of the ship.

I don't.

Swallowing hard, I glance down to see that the deck has changed from being newly scrubbed planks to a single, rough plank.

'Flynn!' I hear Red cry. She must have followed me up on deck. 'You're walking the plank, or staggering the plank, more like!'

'I shee that,' I slur. 'Not good, not good at all.' I stumble and fall onto my backside, only just managing to stay on the plank, which wobbles perilously beneath me. I feel my stomach sink as I catch sight of the treacherous waves crashing below.

'I'd say it's very good!' Drudger grins, edging his way onto the plank in pursuit. 'Saves me the bother of throwing you overboard to feed the sharks.'

I feel a knot of bile rising in my stomach. I know there is nothing I can do. Drudger edges closer and closer. My guts churn harder. Grog and the roll of the ship are proving a lethal mix and I just know I'm going to…

Peeeeuuuuuuuuk!

I vomit a watery missile of bile, biscuit and weevils. It lands on the plank at Drudger's boot.

With a yell, he crashes back onto the plank and
rolls off, only just managing to grab the edge.
He dangles over the dark waves.

I lurch forward past his fingertips, then turn
and fall on my knees.

'Take my hand!'

But Red is right behind me.

'Yer in no position to save anyone,' she says.
'Let me by, Flynn, before yez both end up in
the sea.'

Red helps me, then drags Drudger back onto the plank. I notice we have an audience – the rest of the crew have gathered to watch.

But the drama is over. Drudger slopes off and the last thing I remember is Red yelling after him, something about grog and how we all could have drowned, and then about getting me to my hammock.

CHAPTER SIX
THE MUSEUM

Land Ahoy!

I wake the next morning to Red booming in my ear.

'Do you have to shout? My head hurts.'
I sit up. 'Wait a minute, did you just say...'

Red tips me out of my hammock and I fall on the floor with a thud.

'We've arrived at the Isle of Tut. Come on!'

Forgetting about my headache, I scurry after her up to the deck.

The sun is just coming up behind three huge dark pyramids, silhouetted on the coastline. They rise into the sky, their points jabbing into the streaked clouds of orange and blue. A grey mist skirts each of the pyramids and between them, the murky River Vile meanders down to the sea. I gasp.

'Wow! They look even more awesome in real life.'

At the foot of the tallest pyramid, I can see a town of flat-roofed houses, dotted with palm trees.

'Welcome to the Isle of Tut, and our next mission,' says Red. 'Briggs is looking for you, so you best get a move on. I've got to go, we'll be dropping anchor soon. Oh, and you might want to keep out of Drudger's way.'

Suddenly snippets of my action-packed first day at sea come rushing back to me.

'Don't worry, I plan to. See you later.'

There is a lot to be done before we drop anchor and it seems like an age before the Captain hollers.

'Right, Hudson, you'll pick some men and head for town to pick up supplies for the ship. Briggs, Red, Drudger and Flynn, you'll come with me to the museum.'

My heart sinks. It was too much to hope for that Drudger would have been picked for the supply run. How am I supposed to keep out of his way now?

We make our way along the dusty roads into town. The pyramids loom larger as we walk. It's not long before the museum comes into sight, a white stone building that looks as old as the pyramids themselves. As we enter, a woman hurries out of an office right next to the entrance.

'Oh thank goodness, Captain Watkins, you have come at last. I am Miss Wrinkly, the museum curator.'

Miss Wrinkly, I quickly deduce, does not live up to her name. She is probably the most non-wrinkly person you can imagine. Her face is smoother than the Gypshun mask on display in the entrance hall, and her skin is almost as golden.

The Captain shakes her hand.

'Pleased to meet you, Miss Wrinkly. And don't worry, you done the right thing in sending the parrot. You've now procured the services of a ship full o' the cleverest pirate investigators you'll ever meet.'

'I just can't believe it. The Sceptre of the Pharaohs, especially – it's priceless! Now we might never get it back. The police have been hopeless. They did manage to get here during the raid, but it was a moonless night and it was easy for the thieves to slink off into the darkness.'

'The police are no match for our powers of deduction. Can you take us to the scene of the crime? You haven't touched anything, I hope.' She shakes her head.

'It will take weeks to get things back to normal. They left the place in a right state.'

'Good. Always best not to disturb a crime scene. We'll start by looking for clues.'

'King Tut's Hall on the first floor is where they did the most damage, and in the Rooms of the Royal Mummies.'

We walk along the main hall of the ground floor, which seems to have been overlooked by the burglars. I stare at the exhibits, huge bronze statues, tables, coins and coffins, which Red tells me are called sarcophagi. We walk past a papyrus painting of an ancient Gypshun sailing boat gliding along the River Vile. I wonder if back in the day, there were ancient pirates too...

Miss Wrinkly leads us into a large room that looks like it's been hit by a massive cannonball. Wood splinters from broken cabinets and shattered glass litter the floor.

She looks at Red and me.

'Watch you don't cut yourself on the glass.'

I examine the area around some of the broken cabinets. Bronze spear heads, pots, and figurines have all been left on the floor near

the cabinets. It was as though they had been lifted off, then the cabinets smashed up.

'I'd guess that as well as stealing booty, the thieves were looking for something,' I say.

The Captain glances up from studying a large bootprint with his magnifying glass.

'What makes you think that?'

'These cabinets. I mean, why bother to smash them up? Why not just steal what's inside them? But instead, they've left all the stuff lying around.'

'It's like tipping out the treasure then smashing up the chest,' Red muses.

We get back to work. I notice that Drudger
looks disinterested, poking around, pretending
to look for clues. He picks up something small
and shiny and pops it in his pocket.

Then he drifts over to me, baring his
yellow teeth.

'I haven't forgotten about last night y'know,'
he growls.

'I have. I can't remember a thing.'

He shoves me and I fall
against a cabinet that
topples and breaks
open. Drudger laughs.

'Watch what you're
doing,' the Captain
barks. 'You might be
destroying…'

'…Evidence,' I finish.
'Er, I think I might've just
found some.'

'You have?' Red comes scurrying over.

An old sheet of paper has been concealed inside the hollow bottom of one of the cabinets. The Captain strides over to peer inside.

'What is it?'

Carefully, I pull it out.

'It looks like… a map. Although this edge is uneven, like it's been torn.'

'Part of a map. Maybe that's why the thieves were splitting open the cabinets,' Red says.

The map is yellowed and worn, with a compass in the corner. It depicts a coastline with stick trees, pyramids, and a winding river. There are dots along the shore near a cove, and some letters which make as much sense to me as hieroglyphs.

'Looks like the coastline of the Isle of Tut,' I say.

'Looks like a treasure map,' says Drudger eagerly. The Captain strokes his chin.

'Maybe the thieves found the other half and were looking for this when the police arrived, so they had to make a quick getaway. And if that's the case, then I reckon we need to check out what's so important about it.' He nods at me. 'Well done young Flynn. You've only gone and given us our first lead.'

'Drudger helped.' I grin and he scowls back at me.

We follow the Captain back out to the museum entrance, where we almost bowl over Miss Wrinkly.

'Leaving already?' she asks worriedly. The Captain shows her the map.

'Have you ever seen this before, or do ye know what it could be?'

'No, how curious. It looks like a stretch of our coast. Where did you find it?'

'Hidden in one of the broken cabinets. Reckon we should sail the Hound there now to check it out. Back soon.'

Half an hour later, we are hoisting anchor to set sail for the cove, and hopefully some clues. As we start out, I get the creepiest feeling that we are steering into perilous waters. And no sooner have we sailed round the headland, the Captain lets out a yell.

'Shiver me timbers, I might have known it!'

Up ahead, a dark, menacing sailing ship has dropped anchor in the cove, with a black flag hoisted high on the mizzenmast. A dragon figurehead is on its bow.

'The Scurvy Serpent!' he gasps. 'Might explain that strange bootprint I saw back at the museum.'

'Do you know that ship, Captain?' I ask.

'I know it all right. Every born pirate knows that ship, an' it strikes fear into the best of 'em.

That ship, my boy, belongs to the cunningest,
evilest pirate that's ever sailed the Seven Seas…
Captain Jim-Lad Morihearty!'

CHAPTER SEVEN
CAPTAIN MORIHEARTY

I sense fear spreading round the crew like deck fog, as we sail past the bow of the Scurvy Serpent.

'Steer her in close, Hudson,' Watkins orders. 'I've a mind to have a few words with the Captain of this 'ere vessel.'

'What if they fire on us, Cap'n?' Hudson asks,

his voice quivering.

'Already thought of that one. Hoist the parley flag, Red!'

'What's the parley flag?' I ask Red, following her to the mast.

'Parley is part of the Pirate Code of Conduct that all pirates do their business by. It's like a truce, meaning both ships promise no harm until the parley is over, so they can have a meeting.'

Red hoists the parley flag. It's white, with a black skull and crossbones – a pirate flag in reverse.

'Now we wait for the other ship to respond by hoisting the same flag, that's what the Pirate Code says.'

So we wait. And wait.
And wait. Nothing.

Captain Watkins scans the deck with his telescope.

'Don't see too many crew about,' he says. 'We'll row a jolly boat over to take a look.'

'Looking for me?' a voice booms.

I spin round to see two pirates, one fat and the other skinny, standing on the deck. It's like they just appeared from thin air. Scratch leaps down from the rigging to arch her back and hiss furiously. The Captain draws his cutlass.

'That en't in the rules of parley,' says the tall, thin pirate. He has dark beady eyes, and is clean shaven, with rows of pearly white teeth. He looks part pirate, part shark. Captain Watkins frowns.

'That's Captain Morihearty,' he whispers to me.

'How'd yez board my ship without my knowin' it?' he demands.

'We was in the launch, returning to our ship from the coast, when we saw yer parley flag. Thought you'd be pleased if we dropped by, as it saves you the bother of coming on board the Serpent.' He gestures to the fat pirate. 'This 'ere's me First Mate, Dogbite.'

I notice Drudger stare
admiringly at the two pirates,
his mouth gaping like a fish.

Watkins sheaths his cutlass,
his eyes narrowing.

'Bin a long time, Morihearty. What brings
you to these shores?'

'I could ask you the same thing, Watkins.

Though I reckon
it's probably got
something to
do with all this
pirate investigating
you bin doin' of late?'

Watkins nods and looks
Morihearty in the eye.

'There was a nasty
robbery on this
island a few
nights back.

You wouldn't happen to know anything about it, would you?'

'Never heard about no robbery.' He frowns, glancing at Dogbite, who shrugs. 'Hope ye en't thinking I had anything to do with it. Not me, Watkins. You might be surprised to hear it, but I'm done with pirating. I've turned over a new leaf. Like you done, when you gave up pirating to become an investigator.'

'Is that so?' says the Captain, suspiciously.

'On the straight and narrow now, en't we, Dogbite?' He draws his cutlass, its blade

catching the sun's light. Then he sheathes it again. 'Gone up in the world, I have. I'm more of a collector of arts and antiquities now.'

'Straight as a pirate's hook,' Watkins mutters under his breath. I grin.

'Matter o' fact, the Navy boarded the Serpent only the other day and searched it from top to bottom. Never found a single trace of booty. So rude. Did they give you that sort o' hassle when you gave up pirating, Watkins?'

'For a while yes, until they were sure I was genuine.' Watkins strokes his chin. 'What were you doing on shore?'

'Picking up supplies.'

'Where from?' I ask, louder than I had meant. Morihearty rounds on me.

'Ya got something to say, lad?'

I look into his shark eyes as my heart pounds. 'The... the nearest town is miles away.'

'Lad's right,' says Watkins. 'Coastline's as bare as a ghost ship's galley, nothing more than cliffs and coves round here.'

'Think yer pretty clever, don't yez. Except if yez were really clever, ya wouldn't be wasting yer time parleying with an ol' ex-pirate, when ya could be out there catching the real museum robbers.'

The Captain fixes him with a stare.

'I never told you it was a museum that got robbed.'

I see Morihearty's cheeks redden. 'Don't take a genius to work that out that's where all the treasure is,' he says. 'Besides, it couldn't have been us, as we only sailed into the cove today, and you said the break-in happened a few nights ago.'

'And I only have your word to take for that.'

Morihearty slaps Dogbite on the shoulder, then turns to walk across the deck. 'This parley's over, Watkins. My word is as good as yours. So if ye'll excuse us, we'll be getting' back to our ship.'

He pauses at the top of the rope ladder, gazing at the rigging of the Black Hound.

'The ol' dog is holding together well, Watkins. Ye'll want to keep her that way?'
The Captain scowls.

'Is that a threat?'

Morihearty grins.

'Just a warning. There be dangerous waters out there on the Seven Seas. I'm only telling you to be careful. Goodbye, Captain Watkins.'

And the two men are gone, down the rope ladder to the jolly boat.

As we watch them row back to the Serpent, the Captain turns to me.

'You're pretty brave standing up to Morihearty back there. He'd slit yer gizzard without so much as a second thought. He's a liar of course. Though I do believe the Navy were on his ship.'

'But how come they didn't find anything? Wouldn't he have loads of stolen booty?'

'He's much too clever for them. He'd keep all the booty off ship, buried on islands or stored in towns and cities all over the Seven Seas.'

'Like Baskervile?'

'Baskervile, Bellgravya… You name it. Morihearty's stash stretches across all the known world, and his rotten crimes too. He's like a giant octopus with a tentacle in every sea.'

'But there are only seven seas. Doesn't an octopus have eight tentacles?'

'Aye, lad.' The Captain eyes me, a worried look on his face. 'He has the eighth tentacle behind his back holding a cutlass, ready to get you if you cross him.'

CHAPTER EIGHT
GHOST STORIES

We set a course back along the coast, drop anchor and make for the museum. As soon as we get there, Miss Wrinkly tells us she has been talking to her friend Miss Chatti in Records and Archives, who wants an urgent word with us, the pirate investigators.

It is getting dark and I had thought
we might be calling it a day soon, but the
Captain thinks we should follow this up.
So we climb down several flights of stone
stairways to a labyrinth of passages, lined
with endless rows of files and books.

'Wow, these corridors go on for ever,' I say.
'And they all look exactly the same. How
does Miss Wrinkly's friend find her way about
down here?'

'Hellooooooo! Is
anyone out there?'
The Captain calls.
I hear a faint
whirring noise,
gradually getting
louder. Then, a little
old woman appears,
whizzing towards us on a
moving ladder, which is

secured to a rail running along the tops of the cabinets. It must be Miss Chatti. She stops beside us and steps off, tying back her long grey hair in a ponytail.

'Who are you?' she asks, squinting over the rim of her glasses.

'Watkins, Captain Watkins. And this is Flynn, my cabin boy. Miss Wrinkly said you wanted to see us.'

'Ah, the detective.' She pulls out some files from a shelf and blows the dust off them.

Sneezing uncontrollably, she then coughs and splutters before shoving the files into the shelf below.

'You don't look like a detective to me – more like a pirate.'

'P'raps there's somewhere we can sit down?' the Captain asks, twitching his nose like he's going to sneeze, too.

Miss Chatti leads us to a room, full of more cabinets and chairs. There is a table with dusty books on it. She makes us a cup of tea then joins us around the table.

'Took me back, it did, when Miss Wrinkly told me about the map you found. He worked here, see, as a guard for a few years, after he retired.'

'Who did?' the Captain asks.

'Dr Khan. Good pal of mine who passed away a couple of years ago. Not that he ever guarded much when he was here – he spent

half the time snoozing.
Though we got on like a
house on fire. He was so
funny, always telling jokes
and funny stories. Course
it weren't long till I'd
heard them all before.
I can still remember
some of them.' She
turns to peer at me. 'What
lies at the bottom of the sea and shivers?'

'I don't know,' I answer. 'A nervous wreck.'

Miss Chatti bursts into infectious giggles.
I laugh too, then notice the Captain puff out
his cheeks. So far Miss Chatti isn't making
much sense, and I wonder if the Captain is
losing patience. He clears his throat.

'Miss Wrinkly told us you had some
information for us, something about the map.'

'And I do, at least I think I do. You see you

probably wouldn't think of a cabinet maker as someone with a sense of fun, stuck in a cluttered old workshop hammering bits of wood together all day. He'd be dull as dishwater.'

I stare at the rows of brown files and wonder if Miss Chatti is a bit bonkers.

'So, Dr Khan made all the cabinets upstairs,' I say.

The Captain raises an eyebrow and I hope I haven't spoken out of turn.

She blinks at me with her bright blue eyes.

'Most of them, yes. Except for the cabinets in Mummies and Daggers, oh, and the Royal Rooms, too. He'd have been heartbroken to see them all broken up like that, if he were still alive.'

The Captain strokes his chin.

'Have you any idea why someone would damage them?'

'Maybe,' she says with a conspiratorial smile. 'You see as well as a cabinet maker, Dr Khan was a keen Gyptologist, too. And he wasn't always telling jokes either. No, sometimes he'd tell ghost stories.' I gasp.

'Ghost stories?'

She chuckles.

'Especially when we had to work late, and it was dark outside.'

'What kind o' ghost stories?' Captain Watkins asks.

'About the spirits of the old Gypshun gods, and about their mummies coming back to life. He could translate the ancient manuscripts and inscriptions. His favourite was one about King Tut and his pirate ship. It prophesied that the ship would sail the Seven Seas again one day. And all because of a dark magic hidden in the amulet of the sceptre. The very same sceptre that was stolen from this museum.'

I feel a lump of fear rise in my throat.

The Captain's eyebrows creep up
his forehead.

'Ancient pirates, dark magic, whatever.
Never heard of such things.'

Miss Chatti slides a book across the table.
It is old and battered, with worn, yellow-
brown pages. On the cover, in faded gold
lettering, the title reads:

Prophesies of King Tut
By
Dr Khan

'It's all in here,' she says. 'Dr Khan wrote
it down. Tried to publish it too, but no
publisher would touch it, so he had to make
this little book himself. Though he did
manage to publish a few pamphlets and
articles over the years. Pity really.
You're welcome to borrow it, so

long as you bring it back. Now I sound like a librarian – how very dull of me!'

'I would like to borrow it, please,' I say. 'But you still haven't told us about the map.' She rolls her eyes.

'Ah, of course, the map. I was coming to that. He used to talk about the map a lot. Never showed it to me though. I sometimes wondered if he was making it all up. But one night, he told me he knew where a missing pirate ship was buried, and that he'd drawn a map. He spoke of a river under a pyramid, and secret chambers as big as the museum.

Big enough to contain a ship that would sail again one day. It gave me proper nightmares, it did.'

'So maybe he hid his map in one of the cabinets he made, for safe keeping,' says the Captain.

'And that's what the robbers were looking for,' I add.

The Captain scratches his head.

'One thing I don't understand is if Dr Khan knew where the ship was buried, why didn't he try to find it himself?'

'You mean plan a dig. Oh, but he did,' says Miss Chatti. 'He tried to for years, but could never get the funding. The Museum

Board of Directors would make excuses
about the cost, lack of evidence and even
safety issues, but between you and me,
I think they all thought he was a bit mad.
And I sometimes wonder if they were right.
I mean, if he really was as clever as he made
out, why was he working as a museum guard?
I can't think of anything more…' She pauses,
searching for just the right word.

'Dull,' I finish her sentence.

'Yes.'

The Captain rises to his feet.

'Thanks for your help, Miss Chatti. We'll
not keep you any longer tonight. I'm
sure you've work to be getting on with.'
He gave me a wink. 'Must be very
interesting.' I grin.

'Definitely not dull!'

We make our way back to the
ship. I feel tired. I wonder if the

Captain would call it a day. Did he ever stop? I decide that a pirate investigator's life is a busy one indeed. But I wouldn't have it any other way.

'So, what have we got?' the Captain asks as we walk. 'A break-in and an ancient curse about a Pharaoh's pirate ship. A hidden map, or half a map, showing not buried treasure, but a buried ship. And this mysterious ship is somewhere near where our friend Morihearty just so happens to be sniffing around.'

'Do you think Morihearty knows about the hidden ship and the prophesy?' I ask.

'Can't say for sure, but right now he's Suspect Number One. And first thing in the morning, we're going to find out what that old crook's up to.'

CHAPTER NINE
SNAKES

The next morning, I wake to the sound of hissing. I groan, opening one eye. I had been up before dawn feeling seasick, and had just managed to doze off again. The hissing sounds like one of Fishbreath's pots bubbling in the galley, but my quarters are nowhere near that part of the ship. Next thing, I feel

something crawl over the blanket at my feet.
I open both eyes to see a black oily head and
a flickering forked tongue.

'Snake!' I cry as it opens its mouth,
revealing two needle-sharp fangs. It lunges at
me and instinctively I jerk my legs upwards,
flipping it head-over-tail out of my hammock.

Writhing in protest on the floor, the snake
hisses even louder. Then in a blur of fur and
sharp teeth, something streaks out of the
shadows, clamping the snake between its jaws.

'Scratch! Good job,' I gasp. 'It were

probably poisonous, so you just saved my life.'

Scratch purrs loudly then scampers off with her prey.

Up on deck, Fishbreath pushes past me.

'Cap'n's sick, and most o' the crew besides, and it weren't my biscuits, before ye say it.'

'Wouldn't by any chance be snake bites?'

'Reckon it might be. How'd you know?'

'Cos I just been sharing my hammock with a big ugly one.'

'Red's with the Captain now. She sent me to make sure everyone who isn't sick was up, and on the look-out. Reckon the ship's infested with snakes. Don't suppose you've seen Drudger?' I shake my head, muttering.

'Thankfully no. I'm still keeping out of his way.'

In his quarters, the Captain is lying in bed and looks as white as a ghost.

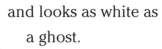

'Will he be alright?' I whisper to Red.

'He'll live,' she says. 'I sucked out the poison, then put a few herbs to help heal the skin. That ol' witch I worked for was a real pain, though she did teach me some useful stuff, too. You OK?'

'I'm fine, thanks to Scratch. Looks like you, me and Fishbreath are the only ones that haven't been bitten.'

'I told Drudger to wake you.'

'He didn't, and Fishbreath hasn't seen him either. How did the snakes get aboard?'
She shrugs.

'Your guess is as good as mine, but I smell a rat.'

'You think it could be someone who doesn't want us snooping around the case of the museum robbery?'

'Ahoy there! Hands off me booty, yez snivellin' sea rats, or ye'll both walk the plank!'

I turn round to see the Captain waving his cutlass wildly from his sick bed.

'What booty?'

'He's delirious!'
Red says, calmly
disarming him.
'We'll put this
out of harm's

way until he's feeling better.'

'How long will he be like that?'

'I don't know. A day, few days maybe.'

'A few days,' I gasp. 'But what about the case? Briggs is second in command, isn't he?'

'He's just as doolally, I'm afraid. Last time I checked on him, he was making squeaking noises and telling everyone he was a dolphin.'

Fishbreath comes bursting in.

'I know I'm not the most useful when it comes to investigating an' all that, but I reckon you should know something.'

'What?' Red says.

'Snitch says he saw Drudger row off in a jolly boat at first light. He had taken a scroll with him. At first I thought Snitch were just talkin' gibberish 'cos of his snakebite, but then

I checked the Captain's desk and found the map is gone.'

'We've got to go after Drudger. But we need someone to steer the ship.'

I look at Red, who is grinning. She tosses the wet towel at Fishbreath.

'Keep the Cap'n nice and cool and give him sips of water.'

'I'm a cook, you know, not a doctor,' Fishbreath protests.

'In times of crisis, it's all hands on deck, Cap'n always says, and if this en't a crisis, then I don't know what is.'

On the half deck, Red stands proudly at the wheel.

'Hoist the anchor, Flynn,' she orders.

Red is actually pretty good at captaining the Hound, and soon we are sailing into the cove. Probably not a good a time to start my own steering lessons though, I decide.

'Look! The Scurvy Serpent has gone,' I say.

'Maybe it's sailed on up the coast, to where the symbols were scribbled on the map.'

We sail further along the coast.

I picture the map in my mind, trying to remember details of the coastline, like the shape of the coves and unusual landmarks on the ground. I spy some jagged rocks at the headland.

'Look! Those rocks are on the map. I'm sure of it. We must be close.'

'Maybe closer than you think,' Red says. 'Look!'

'The Scurvy Serpent!' I gasp. Even though it is a good distance away, there's no mistaking it.

'Keep your distance, Red.'

'Don't worry, I plan to.'

I peer through the Captain's telescope.

'En't a soul on deck. Where are they all? Wait a minute, there's a jolly boat tied up at the stern. It's one of ours!'

'Drudger!' Red snarls.

'No prizes for guessing whose side he's on now.'

'And no doubt he's given Morihearty our map, to match the other half he stole from the museum.' I gasp.

'Morihearty must know about the prophesy, and he wants to find the hidden ship. Maybe for its treasure, or maybe for something else.'

'So where are they now?'

I squint through the telescope at the steep, cliff-backed coastline, then I find what I'm looking for.

'There's a cave, a big one too. And that rocky arch, it's like the one on the map marked with an X.'

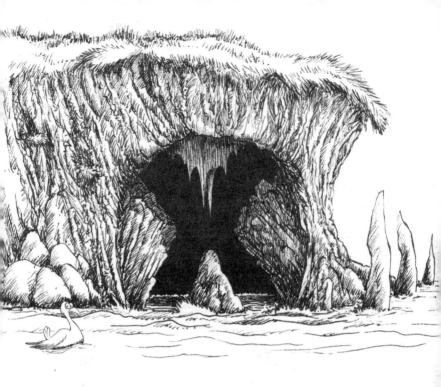

'D'ya think the cave is big enough for a jolly boat?'

'Only one way to find out.'

CHAPTER TEN
INSIDE THE SEA CAVES

Red takes the first turn rowing, while I steer the boat inland toward the cliffs. Then we go further still into the tall cave entrance, that is easily wide enough for six jolly boats.

We enter a massive sea cavern, and I remember what Miss Chatti said about secret chambers as big as the museum.

The waters are calm, but the cavern is
topped by large, menacing rocks that
hang down like suspended cutlass blades.
Some look as though they might fall at any
minute, to pierce the still waters below.

'I've never seen anything like this in my
life. Those dagger-like rocks…'

'Stalactites,' Red says.

'Stalac-whats?'

'Or stalagmites. I get them mixed up.
All I know is, one goes up, and the other
goes down.'

It's dark inside the cavern, and I fumble for
the lantern in the bow of the boat.
'This place is magical,' I say, lighting the lamp.

'D'you think they came this way?' Red asks.

'I'm sure of it. Look, there's a broken oar
floating over there.'

'Maybe it got snagged on a stalagmite,'
Red says. 'That's the kind of rock that grows
upwards… The oar could be from any boat,
but I can't imagine too many other people
would be exploring this cave.'

We row deeper and deeper into the
cavern, our boat lamp flickering. A cloud of
bats dive toward us in a flurry of wing beats.
My heart pounds hard in my ribcage. After a
while, the stalactites are less frequent, and the
banks widen.

'It's like a river, a great underground river
of black water.'

'Brilliant, Flynn,' Red exclaims,
with a nervous grin. 'That's just
what we'll call it.
River Blackwater.'

I'm pretty sure she is

pretending to be brave, but truth be told, I think we are both quaking in our boots. We have no idea where the River Blackwater is taking us, and there are probably scarier critters than bats lurking in the darkness. But worse than that, there's a chance Morihearty and his dastardly crew are somewhere up ahead, ready to ambush us at any minute.

We row silently for a while. The rhythmic sweep of the oar blades through the dark waters is the only sound.

'We've been rowing for ages,' Red says.

'We must be a fair way inland by now.'

I remember the little line on the map. Was it showing the river?

'Can you see what's on that wall of rock?'

Red points.

'Looks like the hieroglyphs at

the museum.'

'Yeah, but what are they doing in here?'

'Reckon the great pyramids will be right above our heads.'

Suddenly, I hear a faint swishing noise. 'Do you hear that?' I ask Red.

'Sounds like rain, heavy rain.'

The noise gets louder, and I notice white bubbles floating towards us.

We row on, until up ahead I see white streaks powering down the rocks, crashing into the river. They are tossing a fine mist into the cavern.

'A waterfall!' I cry.

'It's beautiful,' Red gasps.

'But we can't have reached the back of the cavern.' I frown. 'Where's Morihearty?'

'Maybe he didn't come in here after all. We don't know for sure.'

'But that oar we found… could he have climbed the waterfall?'

'Perhaps he didn't climb it,' Red says. 'What if he went through it?'

'Then let's keep on rowing. There's a gap where the water flow isn't quite as strong, so head for there.'

The roar of the water is deafening as we approach. Battling with the oars, Red just manages to row into a space where the falls are less powerful. I bail out the water with an old bucket, working till my arms are ready to drop off.

Soon we have crossed over to the other side. We find ourselves in another secret cave. This time, it's more like a man-made tunnel hacked out of rock, decorated with some more hieroglyphs.

'Look Red, up ahead, there are lanterns, lots of them. And people.'

'It's Morihearty!'

'Quick, snuff out our light and keep your oar strokes nice and slow. We mustn't be seen.'

We find a spot on the rocky river bank to land the boat, then proceed on foot.

As we creep closer, I see Morihearty and his crew swarming round a long wooden barge. It's smaller than the Hound, with rows of oars jutting out from both sides. On the deck is a long, raised platform, with an ancient golden sarcophagus covered with hieroglyphs. More burial caskets circle the boat, though they look drab compared to the shining sarcophagus.

'It's the missing pirate ship Miss Chatti told us about. Dr Khan was right, it is buried under the great pyramid.'

Now we are close enough to hear

Morihearty shout at Dogbite, his first mate
and the pirate we had met yesterday.
We crouch behind some rocks.

'At last, the lost ship of King Tut!' yells
Morihearty. 'I knew we would find it. Give me
the sceptre, then let the magic begin!'

Dogbite hands the golden sceptre to
Morihearty, who places it inside the golden
sarcophagus. He mutters something, then
takes it out it again.

Red and I stare at each other.

'What's he doing?' Red whispers.

'I don't know.'

Then to my horror, the mummy in the great gold sarcophagus suddenly sits up. Face obscured, with red eyes glowing behind dirty bandages. It stares at Morihearty, then lets out a bloodcurdling wail.

'Tuuuuuuuuuuut!'

I feel an icy chill slither up my spine and my legs turn to jelly.

But worse is to come. All around the boat, the other mummies slowly begin to stir, ancient bones creaking. And in a heartbeat, the deck is transformed from a lifeless funeral barge into a host of grisly bandaged figures, moaning and wailing.

CHAPTER ELEVEN
RISE OF THE MUMMIES

tuuuuuut!!

The mummy wails and climbs out of its coffin, lunging at Morihearty, who jabs back with the sceptre. The crystal at the top of the sceptre glows bright yellow.

The mummy sways forward again, grabbing Morihearty, who twists round and swings the sceptre, knocking the

mummy overboard.

'Tuuuuuuuuuuuuuuuuuut!'
it cries, sinking slowly below the
murky waters.

Heart pounding, I nudge Red.

'Look, the other mummies are bowing to
Morihearty like he's their King now.'

'He's no King, he's completely mad.'

Morihearty stands proudly in front of his
bandaged crew, head held high. He holds
the sceptre aloft, crying, 'He who wields the
sceptre, wields power. Just as these ancient
pirates are bowing to me, soon the Navy and
the whole of the known world will bow to my
authority. I will be King of the Seven Seas!'

'Well what d'you know, looks like I found me a pair o' sneak thieves,' a familiar voice says. I spin round.

'Drudger!' I gasp.

'You two just don't give up, do you?'

Red scowls at him.

'I can't believe you would betray the crew of the Black Hound, Drudger. Pretty low, even by your standards. And I suppose you tried to poison us with those snakes, too?'

Drudger smirks.

'Watkins betrayed the whole lot of us when he gave up proper piratin' for all that stupid detective stuff. Can't even do that right. I'm a better investigator than all o' yez put together. I found a silver button from Morihearty's coat back at the museum, one I'd noticed was missing from his coat when he was on the Hound. So I knew he'd done the break-in, and was probably looking for the map.'

Drudger lunges forward, pushing us down the rocky bank towards Morihearty. The mummy crew are now working around the ship, securing ropes and sweeping the deck.

'Caught these two skulking about in the shadows,' Drudger tells Morihearty.

Morihearty snarls at us.

'How did a bunch of scurvy kids like you find this place? Is Watkins with yez?'

We say nothing.

'They were alone,' answers Drudger.

'Search the cavern and make sure no one else is lurkin' about. And good work, Drudger.'

'Aye, Sir.'

Morihearty turns to me, fixing me with those beady eyes.

'You're that boy from the Hound. The one with the big mouth.'

'So it was you robbed the museum and stole the sceptre,' I say.

'Rob it. Hardly. This wasn't about booty. It was about the sceptre and the map.'

'You won't get away with this. Captain Watkins and the rest of the crew are probably on their way here right now.'

'Your buffoon of a Captain is no match for me. From the day I chanced upon Khan's old pamphlets on the ancient prophesy, I knew this time would come. All I needed was to

find the tomb. And
when Drudger showed
up with the other half
of the map, that was
the final piece of
the puzzle.'

I glance at Drudger,
who is standing on the deck
looking smug.

'Tie 'em up, Drudger, and keep
them out of my way.'

'Be a pleasure, Captain.'

Raising the sceptre, Morihearty shouts
orders at the mummies, who respond
obediently. The cavern echoes with their
grisly groans and morbid wails as they cluster
round the helm of the barge and begin to
push. I stop my ears.

The ancient wooden hull creaks in protest
and I have an awful feeling the whole vessel

134

will collapse. But then it begins to move. Slowly at first, then quickening as it edges towards the sloping bank. With one final push, the barge slides into the river.

And floats!

The mummies clamber aboard, sitting in the rows of wooden seats and lifting the oars with their dirty bandaged hands.

Morihearty stands at the wheel with Dogbite and Drudger.

'Now, let's get out of this cavern,' cries the pirate Captain. 'All this tomb raiding is making me claustrophobic. Sooner I feel the wind blowing on me face, the better.'

Rowing slowly and in unison, the mummies propel the ancient vessel back down the River Blackwater.

'What do you think he plans to do with us?' Red asks.

'Probably set his mummies on us, or make us walk the plank. I don't plan to stick around long enough to find out.'

'Y'mean you have a plan?' Red says.

I shuffle over the deck to pick up a piece

of flint, shaped like an arrowhead. 'This rope looks a bit frayed, Red. If we sit back to back, I might be able to use this flint to cut you free.'

I edge closer to Red, but as I do, the mummy guarding us grabs me and pulls us apart. I feel bile rise in my guts as I smell his rotting bandages, and I'm glad when he flings me away from him across the deck.

The barge ploughs through the waterfall and onwards into the cavern of stalactites.

'Easy as she goes,' Morihearty yells.

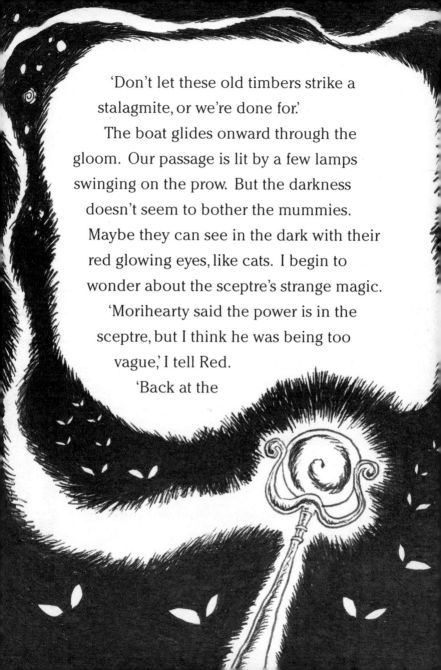

'Don't let these old timbers strike a stalagmite, or we're done for.'

The boat glides onward through the gloom. Our passage is lit by a few lamps swinging on the prow. But the darkness doesn't seem to bother the mummies. Maybe they can see in the dark with their red glowing eyes, like cats. I begin to wonder about the sceptre's strange magic.

'Morihearty said the power is in the sceptre, but I think he was being too vague,' I tell Red.

'Back at the

museum, Miss Chatti said the magic is in the amulet, which is that yellow crystal on top of the sceptre.'

Red nods.

'The witch I used to work for claimed that amulets carry a form of dark magic. She said this magic can be broken if you destroy them.'

'So there's a chance that if we destroy the crystal, then we might wipe out the mummies.'

'We'd have to get the sceptre off Morihearty though, and he doesn't let it out of his sight.'

Up ahead, I can just make out a faint chink of daylight. Soon, the ancient barge is forging through the gap and out into the open sea, for the first time in thousands of years.

'Hoist the sail,' Morihearty orders.

The mummy crew obey, pulling in the oars and raising the sail.

And then I see the Scurvy Serpent, and on the other side of the cove, where we had anchored it, the Black Hound.

Morihearty points the sceptre towards his pirate ship.

'Sail alongside the Serpent, and let's get aboard.'

As we draw closer, the crew of the Serpent throw grappling hooks to pull the barge tight

alongside. The mummies start to clamber aboard, climbing up the ropes.

'What are you going to do with this old barge?' Dogbite asks. Morihearty scowls.

'Set it alight!'

'What?'

'You heard me. Rotten piece of flotsam is barely seaworthy and won't last long against the rough winds and waves o' the Seven Seas. No, this was only ever about the crew of mummies, who won't even flinch at the blade of a cutlass.'

'Even if they did get cut, they're already covered in bandages,' Drudger jokes.

'Set it alight, then sail it into the Black Hound,' Morihearty orders. 'Last thing I need when I take over the Seven Seas is some pesky pirate detective sticking his nose in everywhere. That Captain Watkins is almost as bad as the flamin' Navy.'

CHAPTER TWELVE
SHOWDOWN

R ed and I stare at each other, a look of horror on our faces. What kind of monster is Morihearty? How could he sail a burning ship into a defenceless crew of innocent sailors?

Then I see Dogbite running towards me.

'What about the prisoners, Cap'n?'

'I've a good mind to let them go up in smoke with this old wreck. But you'd better take 'em aboard the Serpent and tie 'em to the mast. I'll figure what to do with them later.'

what to do with them later.'

Next thing, two burly mummies seize Red and me. They grab a rope and swing over the water between the boats, landing with us on the Serpent.

They pin us against the mast, while another mummy fetches some thick rope.

'Red, listen to me,' I whisper. 'Remember to take a deep breath while they're tying us up.'

'What, why?'

'There's no time to explain it to you, just trust me, OK?'

Red looks at me like I've gone crazy.

One mummy grips us by the arms while another binds us tight to the mast. I hope Red hasn't forgotten what I told her.

The chief mummy sets the barge on fire, then strides to the helm to steer it on its deadly trajectory towards the Black Hound. A strong gust of wind billows the single sail, propelling the burning boat toward the anchored Black Hound and its helpless crew. I wonder if Fishbreath is on guard in the crow's nest, then realise that even if they did hoist anchor now, there would not be enough time to sail away from the smaller and faster boat. I don't want to think what will happen if it crashes into the Hound, with the Captain and crew too sick to escape. They are sitting ducks.

The mummy tying us up does not notice that Red and I have taken in deep lungfuls of air.

'What was all that about?' Red splutters, when the mummy leaves.

'A trick I read somewhere, that makes us bigger and the rope looser. Not much, but just enough… so I can get my hands free.'

The trick has bought me enough room to rub the rope binding my wrists against the gnarled mast, until I feel it begin to snag and break apart. Nearly there. Just the thick rope binding us to the mast now. I still have the flint arrow head I found earlier, concealed in my palm. Methodically, I start to carve, the frayed strands of rope falling on my fingers.

Finally, the rope falls to our feet. We are free at last.

'We need to destroy the mummies,' I say. 'Especially the chief mummy who's steering the fire ship into the Hound.'

Red doesn't answer me.

'Red, where are you…?'

'Where d'ya think you are going, ya rancid sea rat?' Morihearty roars, appearing round the mast.

'Stop the fire ship, Morihearty, and call off your evil mummies. You'll never get away with this. The Navy will lock you up and throw away the key.'

The pirate captain extends his arms, like he is about to take a bow.

'Oh, but I think you'll find I just have got away with it. Soon I'll be rid of my old enemy, Watkins, and his crew of interfering idiots.

147

He's so irritating. I'm starting to find you
irritating, too. I should've left you and that
meddlesome girl back there on the fire ship.'

Dogbite scurries over, out of breath.
'Cap'n, I just spotted a couple of ships on
the horizon.'

'Talking of irritating. But I guess that's
perfect. Saves me wasting time looking
for them. I'll have both those Navy ships
for starters.'

I pick up a cutlass and swing it wildly.

'You can't defeat the Navy, Morihearty. Give yourself up and they might spare your life.'

Morihearty laughs.

'What are you doing with that, lad? Bit young to be playing with swords. You'll cut yourself.'

Sensing danger, the mummies all cluster round me like a pack of loyal dogs.

'Seems my new crew don't take kindly to you threatening their King,' snarls Morihearty.

The mummies move in closer. I jab my cutlass at one, but miss my target, tripping over and falling on my face. Struggling to get up, I feel a smelly bandaged arm grab me by the throat and start to throttle me.

Fighting for breath, I see the barge is now engulfed in flames and heading straight for the Hound. The mummies don't seem bothered by the fire and smoke – it's like they are indestructible. No wonder Morihearty wanted a ship full of them.

Desperation overcomes me. It's hopeless. What do I think I can do? Are the mummies too strong?

'Aeeeeeeeeeeeeeeeeeeeee!!!!'

Suddenly, two familiar feet swing through the air toward Morihearty, kicking the sceptre from his grasp. It rolls across the deck.

'Get a move on Flynn!' cries Red, landing beside me.

The mummy is distracted and loosens its grip around my neck. I know I have only seconds to act. With as much strength as I can muster, I duck from the mummy's grasp, wriggling free. Then in a lightning move, I bring my cutlass down on the sceptre, smashing the crystal amulet to smithereens.

With an otherworldly wail, the mummies begin to stagger about the ship, their bandaged bodies darkening to the colour of soot.

They shimmer and fade until they are nothing more than statues of dust, quickly caught up in the wind. A heartbeat later, the deck is thick with swirling clouds of filthy ash, rising upwards to blacken the Serpent's sails.

And the mummies are no more.

I stare out at the barge and see it veer off course, away from the Black Hound. The mummy at the helm has vanished, joining the smoke from the roaring flames.

Morihearty looks like he is about to explode.

'You've ruined everything, ya little bilge rat!' He strides towards me, face reddening, teeth clenched, cutlass raised. 'I'll feed yer guts to the crocs,' he threatens. I stagger backwards, and find to my dismay that I'm following Red onto the plank. Morihearty advances, scowling venomously.

Drudger appears from the gloomy shadows, grinning.

'Pukin' en't gonna get you outta this one, Bones.'

Morihearty growls like an animal,

his beady eyes narrowing.

There's only one way to go.

Red grasps hold of my hand
and shouts,

'Juuuuuuuuuuuumppp!'

We plunge into the cold sea.
I swallow a mouthful of salty water.

'We'll have to swim to the Hound!'
Red splutters.

'I..I'm hopeless at swimming. I'm
not sure I can make it.' Then I catch
sight of something by the curve
of the bow. I rub salt water from
my eyes.

'Wait a minute, maybe we
won't have to. Look, there's a
boat tied up over there.'

We swim for it as Red gasps, 'It's our jolly boat, the one Drudger took to get here.'

As we climb aboard, I hear a clanking noise. The anchor emerges from the sea to be raised up the side of the ship.

'Looks like Morihearty's leaving before the Navy get here.'

'He's not so brave now his mouldy crew have vanished,' Red says.

I grab the oars. 'Let's get out of here.'

I notice Red has something strapped to her back, the few remaining fragments of yellow crystal glinting in the sun.

The sceptre!

CHAPTER THIRTEEN
IN THE END

I watch the fire ship sail out into open sea as we row towards the Black Hound.

Fishbreath helps us off the rope ladder and onto the deck. It feels great to be back on board.

'Snakes alive, where have you two been? You look like you've been shipwrecked and left for shark bait!'

'Worse,' I say. 'We had a run in with a mad pirate who was planning on taking over the Seven Seas with a crew of deadly mummies.'

'Morihearty! Did ya stop him?'

Red points to Morihearty's ship as it sails off into the sunset.

'Aye. We did that alright. For now at least.'

'How's the Cap'n?' I ask.

'He's a lot better. Sitting up in bed now. He'll want to see you. C'mon.'

We follow Fishbreath below deck to the Captain's quarters. Scratch is curled up at

the bottom of the bed. She greets us with a sleepy meow.

Red checks the Captain's snakebite wound, while we tell him everything. I wonder if he thinks we are making it all up, especially the part about the mummies coming to life. But he says he knows it is the truth, as there is no way we could make up something like that. And he was up late last night reading about the prophesy in Dr Khan's book.

Red unties the sceptre and shows it to the Captain.

'We got this back.'

The Captain's mouth falls open.

'You found it!' he gasps. 'Miss Wrinkly will be over the moon.'

'We'll have to explain the broken crystal to her, but it was either that, or Morihearty would be sailing away right now to take over the Seven Seas.'

'Pair o' yez done a brave thing goin' after Morihearty like that. And it sounds like if you hadn't stopped those mummies the way you did, it would have been a disaster. And as for sailing the Hound round the coast, there's a Cap'n in ya, Red.' He grins.

'Thanks, Cap'n, but I'll stick to climbing the rigging for now,' Red says. The Captain nods.

'We can pass on what we know about the robbery to the Navy, though I know Morihearty will find a way to wriggle out of it. He's like a jellyfish, has a knack for slippin' out o' yer hands.'

159

'Still can't believe Drudger would cross us like that,' Red glowers.

'It's a shame about Drudger,' the Captain says, looking sad. 'He weren't much more than a kid, yet he already had too much of the old piratin' ways in him to change. Had a hunch the lad weren't cut out for investigating, but I never had him down as a traitor.'

'Even less hope for him, now he's hooked

up with a villain like Morihearty,' I say. Though part of me is secretly glad I won't have to worry about keeping out of Drudger's way on the Hound anymore.

The Captain strokes his chin.

'What I want to know is how come you two didn't get bitten by the snakes?'

'I fell asleep in the crow's nest,' Red explains. 'Guess snakes en't that big on climbing masts.'

'I got Scratch here to thank,' I say, giving her a rub between the ears. 'She took out the snake that attacked me with a single pounce.'

The Captain grins.

'Well I'm glad you're both OK, 'cos I bin thinking about that week's trial, Flynn. I've decided to cut it to half a week, which I believe is now over.'

I stare at him speechless, with my heart fluttering.

'Job's yours, Flynn, if you'll take it.'

'Thank you, Captain Watkins. I'd like that very much.'

Fishbreath appears in the doorway, holding a tray of bread, fruit and cups of water.

'Figured yez'll be hungry after saving the Seven Seas.'

We eat the grub which, surprisingly, isn't too bad, with not a weevil in sight. Warily though, I sniff my cup to make sure it isn't grog.

'I propose a toast to our new cabin boy and pirate investigator,' the Captain says, raising his cup.

'To Flynn!' they all chorus.

Afterwards, Red and I check on the rest of the crew and are happy to find everyone is on the mend. Then we walk back up on deck. I lean on the rails, looking out over the Gypshun Sea.

'I've been thinking. You still haven't told me what happened to the last cabin boy.'

'The last cabin boy was Drudger.'

'What, you're kidding! So nothing happened to him, really?'

'He grew up. Or didn't, if you know what I mean. To grow up you need to act your age, and he certainly doesn't.'

I start to think about Drudger, and why he would choose to work for a scoundrel like Morihearty, when Red taps me on the shoulder, shouting, 'Last one to the crow's nest is an old peg leg!'

'Wait, I… I…' I put a hand to my mouth and stagger past her, towards the mast.

'Flynn. What's wrong? Is the seasickness back?'

'No.' I take my hand away from my wide grin, to scramble up the ladder. 'But thanks for the head start.'

The End